Max's 4 Questions

Grosset & Dunlap

To Lauren and Allie, who always ask the questions—B.B.
For Mom—B.H.

GROSSET & DUNLAP
Published by the Penguin Group
Penguin Group (USA) Inc., 375 Hudson Street, New York, New York 10014, U.S.A.
Penguin Group (Canada), 10 Alcorn Avenue, Toronto, Ontario, Canada M4V 3B2
(a division of Pearson Penguin Canada Inc.)
Penguin Books Ltd, 80 Strand, London WC2R ORL, England
Penguin Ireland, 25 St Stephen's Green, Dublin 2, Ireland
(a division of Penguin Books Ltd)
Penguin Group (Australia), 250 Camberwell Road, Camberwell, Victoria 3124, Australia
(a division of Pearson Australia Group Pty Ltd)
Penguin Books India Pvt Ltd, 11 Community Centre, Panchsheel Park, New Delhi - 110 017, India
Penguin Group (NZ), Cnr Airborne and Rosedale Roads, Albany, Auckland 1310, New Zealand
(a division of Pearson New Zealand Ltd)
Penguin Books (South Africa) (Pty) Ltd,
24 Sturdee Avenue, Rosebank, Johannesburg 2196, South Africa

Penguin Books Ltd, Registered Offices: 80 Strand, London WC2R ORL, England

ISBN 0-448-44121-7   10 9 8 7 6 5 4 3 2 1

Max's 4 Questions

By Bonnie Bader • Illustrated by Bryan Hendrix

Grosset & Dunlap

Max Morris lived in a four-story house. He was one of four brothers, and had four dogs, four parakeets, and four goldfish.

Max was the youngest in his family. He was even younger than the goldfish.

It was always very busy in Max's house—very busy and very noisy.

Today, it was especially busy at Max's house, and Max was very curious.

"What is everyone doing?" he asked.

No one answered him.

"Why are you setting the table?" Max asked again, louder this time. Still, no one answered him.

"I said, what's going on?" Max yelled.

This time, Max's mother answered. "We're getting ready for the Passover Seder," she told him.

Max looked at her and didn't say anything.

"Passover is when we remember the Jewish people's exodus from Egypt," Max's mother said.

"*Exodus?*" Max asked. "What in the world are you talking about, Mom?"

"During the Seder, we will tell the story about how the Jews fled Egypt after being slaves there for many years," she replied.

"But—" Max was about to ask another question, but his mother stopped him.

"I'm sorry, honey, but I really don't have time for any more questions right now. Please put the napkins on the table."

Finally, all the plates were on the table.
All the silverware was in its place.
All the napkins were folded. And all the wine glasses were out.
The doorbell rang.

"I'll get it!" Max shouted.

But Max's brother Marc beat him to the door.

In walked Max's four aunts. Max got four pinches on his cheek.

In walked Max's four uncles. Max got four pats on his head.

In ran Max's four cousins. Max was nearly knocked over four times!

Soon, the family was seated around the table.

"What do we do now?" Max asked.

No one answered him. Max looked around. Everyone had opened up their books, called *Haggadahs*. Everyone was quiet.

Max waited. "What do we do now?" Max asked in a louder voice.

Instead of answering him, Max's father began to read from the Haggadah. First, he said the *Kiddush*, which is the blessing over the wine. Everyone drank a glass of wine. Max drank a glass of grape juice.

"Can I have some more?" Max asked.

"Yes," Uncle Dave said. "Tonight everyone will drink four glasses of wine or juice."

The Seder continued. Everyone washed their hands, and then parsley was passed around the table. Max watched as his family said a prayer, and dipped the parsley into saltwater.

After that, Max's dad lifted up a plate of matzos.

"What are you doing?" Max asked.

But Max's father did not answer.

"I said," Max spoke up louder. "What are you doing?"

"I am breaking one of the matzos for the *afikomen*," his dad explained.

"*Afikomen?*" Max asked.

"Yes, I will hide that piece of matzo and later you and your brothers and cousins will try to find it. Whoever finds it gets a prize."

Max smiled. That sounded like fun.

All of a sudden, Max realized that his entire family was staring at him.

Max touched his head. Was something in his hair?

Max picked at his teeth. Did he have a piece of parsley stuck in them?

"It's your turn," Max's brother Moe prompted.

Max looked confused.

"The youngest person asks the four questions," Max's dad said.

Max looked around. *He* was the youngest person at the table!

Max sat up straight in his chair. "Why is this night different from all other nights?" he shouted.

"Max, dear," Aunt Sally said. "Why are you shouting?"

"Because it's hard to get people around here to hear me!" Max said.

Everyone laughed. "Well, tonight we're *all* listening," Max's dad said.

Max continued with the first question.

"On all other nights, we eat either leavened bread or matzo. Why on this night, do we eat only matzo?"

Max stopped and looked around.

"Go on," Max's mother urged. "We'll answer all four questions at the end. I promise."

"On all other nights, we eat all kinds of herbs. Why on this night, do we eat bitter herbs?

"On all other nights, we do not dip herbs at all. Why on this night do we dip them twice?

"On all other nights, we eat sitting up. Why on this night do we eat our meal reclining?"

"*Now* we will answer your questions," Aunt Andrea said.

"And by doing so, you will learn the story of Passover," Uncle Tim added.

"The matzo reminds us that when the Jews left the slavery of Egypt, they had no time to bake their bread. They were in such a hurry that the dough had no time to rise," Max's dad explained.

"On their journey, the dough baked in the hot sun into hard crackers called matzo," Max's mom added.

Max picked up a piece of matzo. "Oh, I see," Max said. "This matzo is very flat."

"We eat the bitter herbs, or *maror*, to symbolize the bitterness the Jewish people felt when they were slaves in Egypt," Max's brother Marc explained.

"And during the Seder, each person takes a bite of the bitter herbs, so they can taste the bitterness," Max's brother Moe continued.

"And we should always remember that we were slaves in Egypt," Max's dad added.

"The *maror* also reminds us of the bitter and cruel way the pharaoh treated the Jewish people," Uncle Dave said.

Max picked up a piece of *maror* and took a bite. "This sure is bitter!" he exclaimed.

"Today, we should be happy that we are not slaves. We are free," Max's dad told everyone.

"Today, we dip the bitter herbs into *charoset* to remind us how hard the Jewish slaves worked in Egypt," Max's father continued. "The chopped apples and nuts look like the clay the slaves used to build the pharaoh's cities, as it says in Exodus," Aunt Andrea added.

"And then we dip again. We dip parsley into saltwater. The parsley reminds us that spring is here and new life will grow," Aunt Karen explained.

"But the saltwater has a sadder meaning. It reminds us of the tears that the Jews shed when they were slaves in the land of Egypt," Uncle Josh added.

"And tonight, we eat in a reclining position to relax. We are no longer slaves. We do not belong to anyone except to ourselves. So tonight, we deserve to take care of ourselves," Max's dad said, leaning back in his chair.

"And now we have answered all of your questions," Max's brother Marc said.

But Max did not look happy. "What's wrong?" his brother Matt asked

"I have one more question," Max said.

"But you're only supposed to ask four," Max's brother Moe said.

"Well here's one more," Max announced. "When do we eat?"

Everyone laughed. "When we finish the first part of the Seder, we can eat," Max's mom said.

"Right after we eat the *Korech*, or the *Hillel Sandwich*, we can eat our meal," Max's dad explained.

"What's that?" Max wanted to know.

"That is when we eat the *maror* and *charoset* together with some *matzo*," Max's mom explained.

Before Max knew it, the first part of the Seder was over, and the meal was finally served.

Max stood up on his chair and shouted, "I have one more question!"

This time, everyone let him ask.

"What's for dessert?"

"The *afikomen* is for dessert," Max's dad explained. "I have hidden it somewhere in the house. Whoever finds it gets a prize."

Max, his three brothers, and four cousins all ran from the table.

In two minutes, Max returned. He had found the *afikomen*. His father gave him a dollar and a book about Passover.

"I don't have to ask what we do next," Max announced. "Dessert!"

Use these stickers to decorate your very own Seder plate!

Use this key for help:

Beitzah = Egg
Charoset = Chopped apples and nuts
Chazeret = Bitter vegetable (celery)

Karpas = Parsley
Maror = Bitter herbs
Zeroa = Roasted shankbone

Use the rest of the stickers to set the Passover Table. Chag Sameach!